To bottoms. All shapes, all sizes.

K.G.

For my super niece, Juliet.

N.D.

First published 2015 by Macmillan Children's Books,
an imprint of Pan Macmillan,
a division of Macmillan Publishers Limited
20 New Wharf Road, London N1 9RR
Associated companies throughout the world
www.panmacmillan.com

ISBN: 978-1-4472-7990-7 (HB)
ISBN: 978-1-4472-7991-4 (PB)

ZIPPO
THE SUPER HIPPO

KES GRAY   NIKKI DYSON

MACMILLAN CHILDREN'S BOOKS

"I wish I was super," said Zippo the hippo
to his best friend Roxi the oxpecker.
"I think you are super," said Roxi.

"I mean I wish I had a super power," said Zippo.

"What sort of super power?" asked Roxi.

"Something exciting!
Something amazing!
Something BIG!" said Zippo.

"Everyone has a super power," said Roxi.
"You just have to work out what yours is."
"What's your super power?" asked Zippo.

"I can stand on no legs," said Roxi.

"I can't even stand on three legs," said Zippo.

"You do have a rather large bottom," said Roxi.

"Is plodding a super power?" said Zippo.
"I'm really good at plodding."

"Not really," said Roxi.

"Is getting muddy a super power?" asked Zippo.
"I'm brilliant at getting muddy."

"Not exactly," said Roxi.
"What else can you do?"

SPLOSH!

"I'm good at swimming," said Zippo.
"And splishing and sploshing and splashing."

"There's nothing very super about
splishing and sploshing and splashing," said Roxi.
"How about flying? Have you ever tried flying?"

"I haven't even thought about flying," said Zippo.

"Then you should!" said Roxi. "Flying is so easy,
I've been doing it ever since I was an egg!
Just imagine how super it would be if you could fly!"

"You're right!" said Zippo. "If I could fly, I could get a super cape and some super boots and I could fly around the world being **Zippo the Super Hippo!**"

"In that case, follow me," said Roxi excitedly. "It's time for your very first flying lessons!"

Zippo climbed to the edge
of a very high waterfall,

flapped his arms
like Roxi,

and jumped!

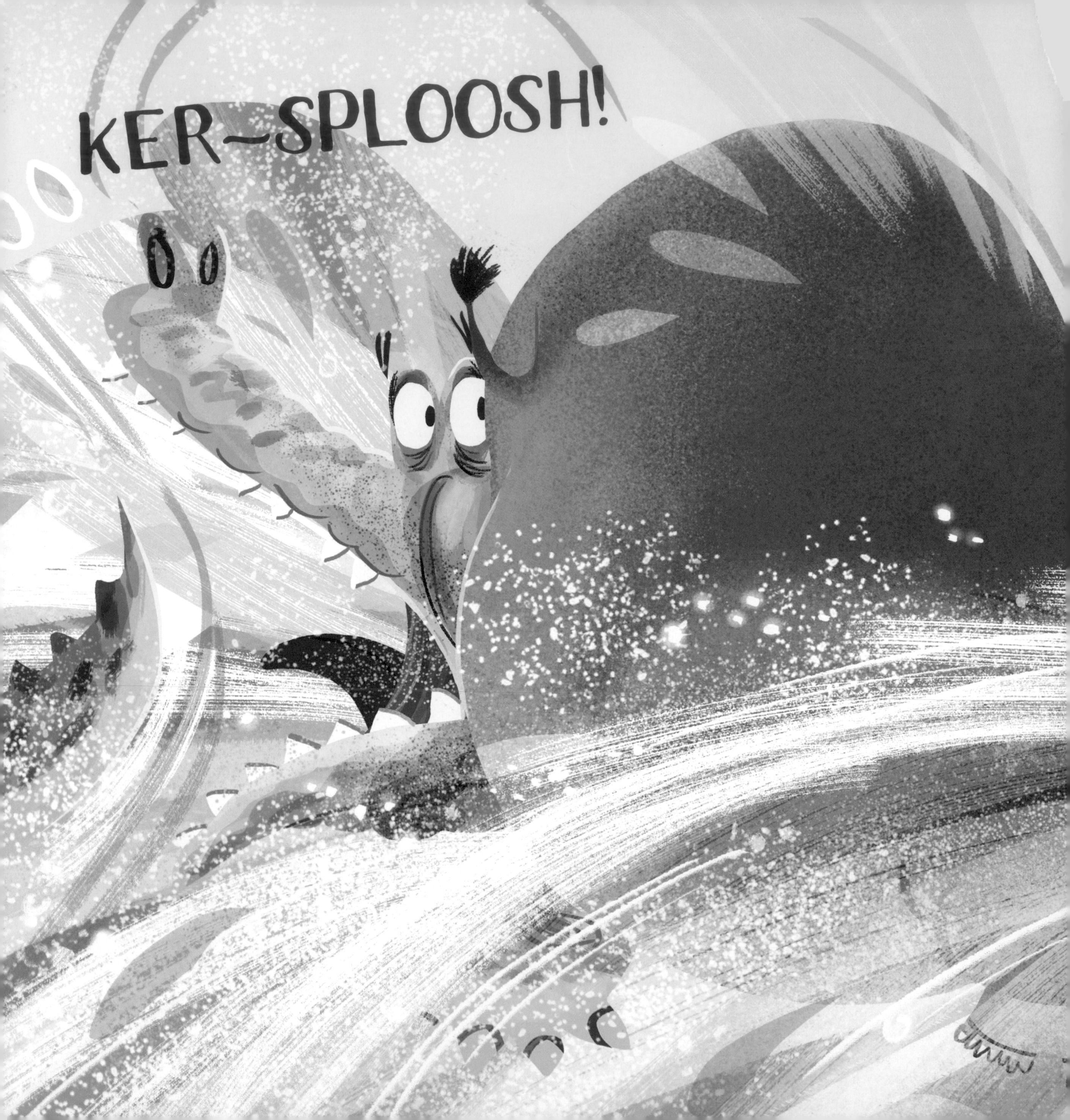
KER-SPLOOSH!

QUACK!

Zippo climbed to the top of a very tall tree, quacked like a duck,

and jumped!

Zippo climbed to the top
of a very steep cliff,
squawked like a vulture,
and jumped!

SQUAWK!

"I don't think flying is really my thing," said Zippo.
"No, but landing is!" said Roxi. "Did you see what
happened each time you landed?"

"I squashed someone,"
said Zippo.

"You didn't just squash 'em," said Roxi,
"You got 'em with your bottom!"
"I got 'em with my bottom?" said Zippo.
"YOU GOT 'EM WITH YOUR BOTTOM!" said Roxi.

"You came out of the sky in your super
hippo costume and you got 'em with your
super hippo bottom!"

"SO I DID!" said Zippo.

"You're not a super hippopotamus, **Zippo**," said Roxi.
"You're a super hippobottomus!"
"SO I AM!" said Zippo.

"This could be the start of something big!" said Roxi.
"How **big**?" said Zippo . . .

"SUPER BIG!" said Roxi.